HELLO, I AM MAX!

from Sydney

Hello, I am Max from Sydney! Come inside to meet my family and my friends...

Stéphane Husar
Illustrated by Mark Sofilas

www.av2books.com

Go to **www.av2books.com**, and enter this book's unique code.

BOOK CODE

N194486

AV² by Weigl brings you media enhanced books that support active learning.

First Published by

abc melody™

Your AV² Media Enhanced book gives you a fiction readalong online. Log on to www.av2books.com and enter the unique book code from page 2 to use your readalong.

AV² Readalong Navigation

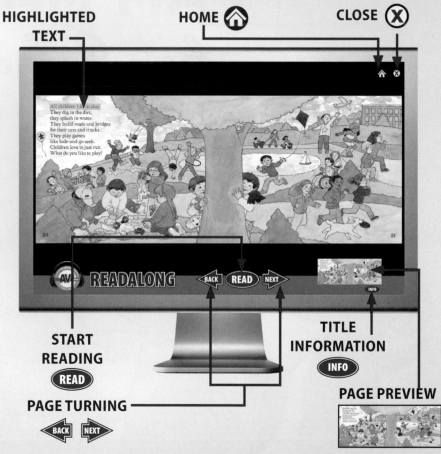

HIGHLIGHTED TEXT

HOME

CLOSE

START READING
READ

PAGE TURNING
BACK **NEXT**

TITLE INFORMATION
INFO

PAGE PREVIEW

Published by AV² by Weigl
350 5th Avenue, 59th Floor New York, NY 10118
Websites: www.av2books.com   www.weigl.com

Printed in the United States of America in North Mankato, Minnesota
1 2 3 4 5 6 7 8 9 0 18 17 16 15 14

042014
WEP080414

Library of Congress Control Number: 2014937153

ISBN 978-1-4896-2250-1 (hardcover)
ISBN 978-1-4896-2251-8 (single user eBook)
ISBN 978-1-4896-2252-5 (multi-user eBook)

Text copyright ©2009 by ABC MELODY.
Illustrations copyright ©2009 by ABC MELODY.
Published in 2009 by ABC MELODY.

ABC MELODY Éditions
26, rue Liancourt 75014
Paris, France

Contents

My name is Max.
I am seven years old.
I live in Sydney, the largest city in Australia.
Sydney has a beautiful harbor, green parks
and fantastic beaches.

4

a city

a harbor

a beach

a park

5

In Sydney, we have two beautiful monuments:
the Harbour Bridge and the Opera House.
The Opera House looks like a sailing boat.
Which monument is the Opera House?

Sydney Harbour Bridge

Sydney Opera House

a sailing boat

Australians love the sea and the beach.
Look at all the surfers and swimmers!
I love to play in the waves with my friends.

the sea

a surfer

a swimmer

a wave

my friends

9

I live with my family in a small house with a big backyard.
I have one sister and two cats. There are many birds
in the backyard. How many birds can you see?

a house

a backyard

my sister

my cats

a bird

My mom is a violinist. She plays the violin in an orchestra, sometimes at the Opera House.
My dad is a postman. He rides a bike all day.
His dream is to ride in the Tour de France!

my mom

my dad

a violin

a bike

a postman

Here are Fred and Misty, our cats.
They are always together.
They love to play with the birds and
sometimes they climb up the trees.
Fred and Misty love to sleep, too.

to climb

a tree

to sleep

I love to go to school. We learn a lot of interesting things there. Here is my best friend Jerrawa. His name means "goanna" in his aboriginal language. A goanna is a large lizard. Jerrawa is very clever!

a school

to learn

a goanna

clever

17

At school, we learn Italian.
- Buongiorno!
It means "hello".
I can say "hello" in many languages.

ni hǎo
Bonjour
Buongiorno
Hola
Guten Tag
Salam

Nǐ hǎo!

Bonjour!

Buongiorno!

¡Hola!

Guten Tag!

Ahlan!

Australians love sport: footy, rugby, cricket, soccer, swimming, tennis. I like to play footy with my friends. Footy is an Australian sport. Jerrawa is the best footy player at my school.

footy

cricket

soccer

cycling

swimming

21

Dad plays the guitar. He thinks he is a rock star!
My sister Kate wants to be an international singer.
I would like to play the didgeridoo in a band with Jerrawa.
Do you know this instrument?

a guitar

a singer

a band

a didgeridoo

a rock star

Every Sunday, Dad and Mom invite their friends for a barbecue in the backyard. Dad loves his barbie and cooks all sorts of things on it: meat, fish, vegetables...
Yum! Fred and Misty love the barbie!

a barbecue (a barbie)

meat

fish

vegetables

to cook

During the summer holidays, we go camping in the bush. I love to sleep in the tent. There are all sorts of Australian animals in the bush: kangaroos, koalas, possums, wombats, kookaburras.
Find the possum on this page.

summer

a tent

the bush

a kangaroo

a koala

a possum

Christmas in Australia happens in the summer, so we don't get snow like in Europe. Here in December, January and February, it is very hot. I think Santa Claus doesn't wear his big coat when he comes to Australia. He probably wears his swimmers and goes surfing...

Christmas

snow

Santa Claus

swimmers
(swimming trunks)

a coat

29

That's it! The visit is over!
I hope to see you soon in Sydney. Goodbye!

Goodbye!

31